My Father's Boat

by Sherry Garland
illustrated by Ted Rand

Scholastic Press　•　New York

FOR MY FATHER,
WHO CAUGHT A 30-POUND
YELLOW CATFISH IN '64

— S.G.

TO BETH AND JACK BAAKE

— T.R.

Text copyright © 1998 by Sherry Garland. Illustrations copyright © 1998 by Ted Rand.
All rights reserved. Published by Scholastic Press, a division of Scholastic Inc.,
Publishers since 1920. SCHOLASTIC and SCHOLASTIC PRESS and associated logos are trademarks
and/or registered trademarks of Scholastic Inc.

LIBRARY OF CONGRESS CATALOGING-IN-PUBLICATION DATA

Garland, Sherry.
My father's boat / by Sherry Garland ; Ted Rand, illustrator.   p.   cm.
Summary: A Vietnamese-American boy spends a day with his father on his shrimp boat,
listening as he describes how his own father fishes on the South China Sea.
ISBN 0-590-47867-2
[1. Fathers and sons — Fiction. 2. Vietnamese Americans — Fiction. 3. Fishers — Fiction.]
I. Rand, Ted, ill. II. Title.
PZ7.G18415My 1998 [E] — dc21   97-19021 CIP AC

10 9 8 7 6 5 4 3 2 1   8 9/9 0/0 01 02 03
Printed in Singapore   46
First edition, May 1998

Book design by Marijka Kostiw
The display type was set in Erazure. The text type was set in Galliard.
Ted Rand's illustrations were rendered in acrylics, watercolor, and chalk on rag stock.

AUTHOR'S NOTE

Beginning in 1975, after twenty years of civil war,
about two million South Vietnamese fled their
homeland, seeking new lives in other countries.
The majority settled in the United States, and many
now live in coastal communities along the Gulf of
Mexico. There they carry on the fishing traditions
of their ancestors.

"When you are young, you need your father;

when you are old, you need your son."

— VIETNAMESE PROVERB

Early one morning, while the sun still sleeps,
I ride with my father down to the fishing docks.

Rows of shrimp boats stand out
like black skeletons against the sky,
bumping softly among the piers.
Lights flicker everywhere, and over the water
men's voices float, deep and hoarse,
as if they haven't drunk their morning coffee yet.

My father holds my hand as I climb on board his boat,
for the wooden deck is slippery and the water is cold.
I sit beside him on the pilot's seat and toot the horn.
Someone answers back, but we don't know who;
all the boats look alike, shrouded in morning fog.

My father's boat slices through the misty air
behind a dozen other shrimp boats
tipped with blinking red lights.
The swirling fog is scary,
but my father says it is only dragon's breath
and will bring us good luck today.

Over quiet waters we glide
until the shore is far away,
and no one else is near.
The whispering wind and slapping waves
and soft *chug chug* of the engine
are the only sounds around us.

I've never been out this far before;
the water looks so deep and dark and the shore so far away.
It feels lonely out on the sea,
but my father says that is part of a fisherman's life —
being alone with the ocean and sky
and creatures living below,
and alone with your memories.

When I lean over the rail to watch the glowing jellyfish,
the mist tingles my face like cool, wet fingers.

My father's hands are strong and hard
from years of hauling nets.
His face is brown and cracked
from squinting out the rays
of ten thousand suns rising and sinking
over the ocean.
His rubber boots
make squishy noises on the deck
and so do mine as I walk behind him.
He gives me the baseball cap from his head
to shade my eyes
from the dazzling morning sun
that dances on the water.

The first catch of the day is good.
My father works as fast and as hard as he can.
He shows me how to fill ice chests with shrimp to sell
and how to shake angry crabs from the nets
and chase them over the deck.
We save some fish for my mother to cook
and some for my aunts and uncles and cousins in town.

At lunchtime we stop to eat cold rice and sip cups of hot tea
while we watch the dolphins playing in the ocean.
My father sings songs he learned in Vietnam,
and he teaches me the words.
He tells me about the mountains and rivers
and fields of waving green rice
and graceful sampans that glide along the shore.
But soon he gets a sadness in his eyes.

"Your grandfather is a fisherman, too," he says,
"on the South China Sea.
He taught me all that I know
and all that I am teaching you.
But when war came to our little village
on the other side of the world,
he could not leave the land he loved,
and I could not stay."

I wonder if my grandfather's hands are strong and callused, too.
Or if he sings to the dolphins the way my father does.
I wonder if he thinks of us while he sips his steaming tea
or while he casts his nets over the water.

"What does my grandfather look like?" I ask.

"Once he was young and strong," my father says,
"but I haven't seen him for over twenty years.
His hair must be gray by now and his eyes growing dim."

"Twenty years is such a very long time.
Do you think Grandfather still remembers you?"

"I know he does.
A father never forgets his children,
no matter how far away they are,
or how long they are gone.
The heart doesn't count the years."

"Do you miss him, too?"
Maybe I ask too many questions,
but my father doesn't seem to mind.

"Yes," my father replies with a heavy sigh.
"More than the mountains and rivers,
more than the waving fields of rice."
He sighs again.
"Someday I will go back and take you
to meet your grandfather.
I will show you his beautiful boat,
and together we will cast our nets
into the South China Sea.
I will show him how well you have learned
the lessons of a fisherman."

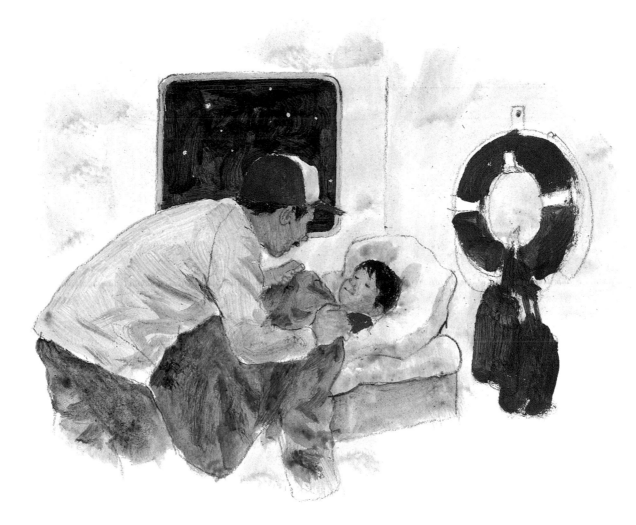

My father works hard the rest of the day
and all night, too, under the starry skies.
I try to keep up with him but my eyelids
are as heavy as curtains of lead.
He lays a pillow on the cabin bench
and covers me with his coat.
It smells like fish and sweat, but I don't mind.

The last stars are fading through heaven's dusty veil
and the laughing seagulls are once more on the wing
when my father's boat glides back into the harbor.
My hands are stinging and my arms are aching,
and I think of crawling into his pickup.
The cushion will feel soft, and I know
I will be asleep before we reach home.

"You did well, son," my father says.
"Someday you will be a great fisherman."

I wonder if my grandfather said those same words
to my father when he was a boy like me.
I wonder if I will say the same thing to my own son one day.
I hope I will never have to sail away to another land
and leave my family behind.

On the long road home, I lean on my father's arm
and soon drift off to sleep.
I dream that we are together —
my grandfather, my father, and I —
out on the lonely sea in my father's beautiful boat.